Puppy Mudge Finds a Friend

By Cynthia Rylant

Illustrated by Suçie Stevenson

READY-TO-READ

ALADDIN

New York   London   Toronto   Sydney

ALADDIN PAPERBACKS
An imprint of Simon & Schuster Children's Publishing Division
1230 Avenue of the Americas, New York, NY 10020
Text copyright © 2004 by Cynthia Rylant
Illustrations copyright © 2004 by Suçie Stevenson
All rights reserved, including the right of reproduction in whole or in part in any form.
ALADDIN PAPERBACKS, READY-TO-READ, and colophon are registered trademarks of
Simon & Schuster, Inc.
Also available in a Simon & Schuster Books for Young Readers hardcover edition.
Designed by Lucy Ruth Cummins
The text of this book was set in Goudy.
The illustrations were rendered in pen-and-ink and watercolor.
Manufactured in the United States of America
First Aladdin Paperbacks edition November 2005
10 9
ISBN-13: 978-0-689-83982-5 (hc.)
ISBN-10: 0-689-83982-0 (hc.)
ISBN-13: 978-1-4169-0369-7 (pbk.)
ISBN-10: 1-4169-0369-0 (pbk.)

This is Puppy Mudge.
He lives with Henry.

Mudge likes it.

He likes a lot of things.

He likes chew toys.

He likes crackers.

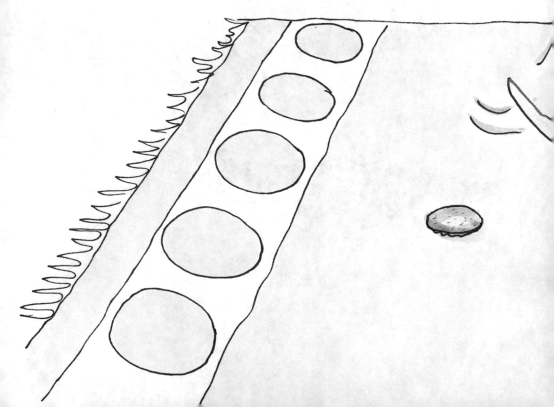

He likes to drool.

(Mudge drools a lot.)

Mudge also likes cats.

Mudge found a cat friend.

Her name is Fluffy.

Mudge and Fluffy play.

Fluffy runs.

Mudge runs.

Fluffy hides.

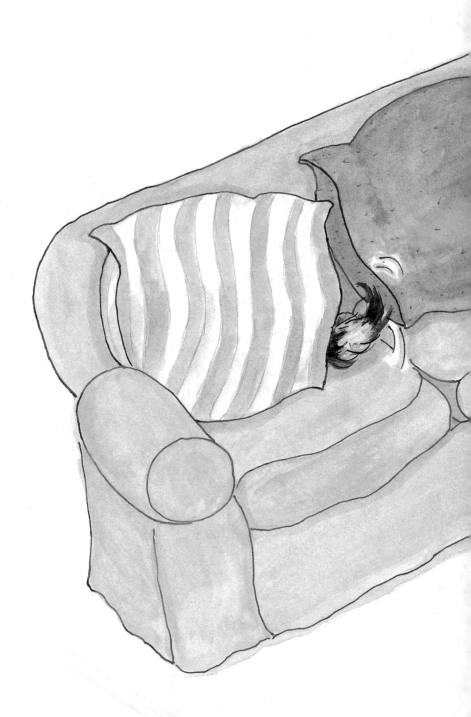

Mudge hides.

Fluffy climbs.

Mudge does not.

Fluffy and Mudge play and play.

Then they rest.

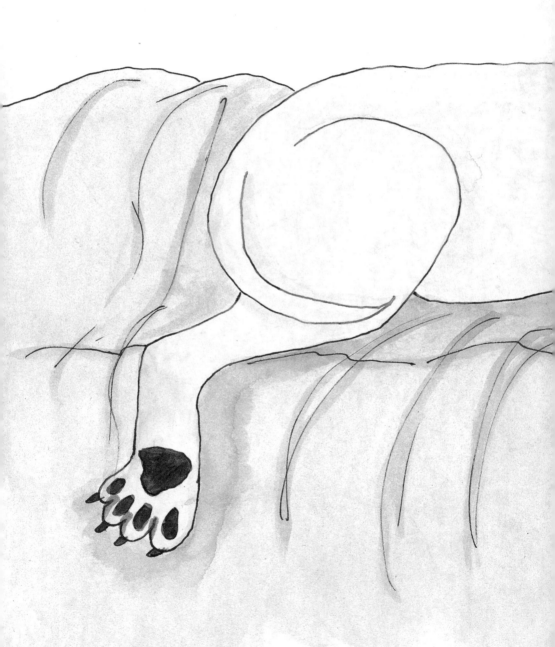

Fluffy purrs.
Mudge snores.

Friends.